W9-BVO-023

RELEASED BY DETROIT PUBLIC LIBRARY

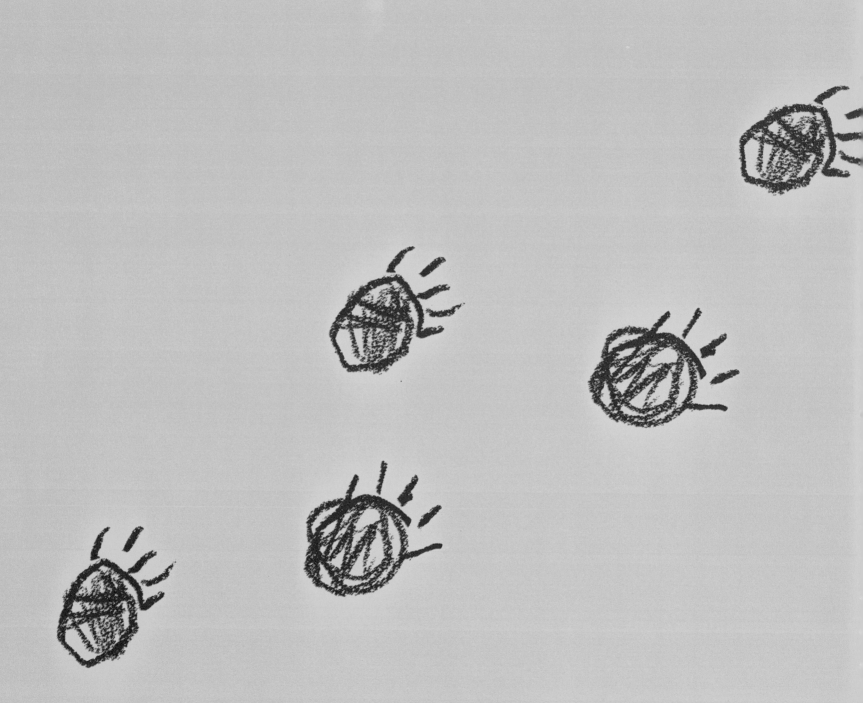

YOU'RE A
BEAR

For Lenorala
        —M.J.

For Tyler
        —S.J. & L.F.

YOU'RE A BEAR

by
Mavis Jukes

paintings by
Steve Johnson and **Lou Fancher**

Alfred A. Knopf   New York

You're a gruff bear, with fleas—
a grump, with a hump between your shoulders.
Scramble from your hidden ledge—
hidden by a bramble hedge—
and squeeze between the boulders.

Ramble through the midnight breeze.

Then—freeze!

You're a bold bear

with a nose as cold as cheese.

Slyly rise up on your toes.
Sniff for owl in the skies—
whiff for mountain goat or moose on the loose
or lynx on the prowl.

Or bees in the trees . . .

Thrash a clump of shrubs for berries!

Rip up rotten logs for grubs!

Check your feet and paws.

There's a chance that

in your fur might

be a termite.

Nibble ants between your claws.

Wish for fish. Stand in the sand
by a stream.
In a pool you'll see reflections of your drool.
You'll see floppy lips—and underneath,
scary teeth that gleam and glimmer.

Above your ears the moon will tip and sink into
a cloud and shimmer
as you dip and drink. And dunk your snout.
Shake those hairy hips to spook the trout!
Then drip and dribble out.

You're a huffy bear. You've missed fish—but
had a wash.
So now you're a fluffy bear.
And all the moonlit meadow grass is yours to
squish and squash.

Spin and tumble.

Sit and sing, or grumble.

Lie back and rest.

Above your furry chest

stars wink.

Dawn leaks blurry shades of peach

and streaks of pink. The moon fades.

Yawn. S ~ t ~ r ~ e ~ t ~ c ~ h those toes!

Reach above your mighty nose and tongue!

You're a tired grizzly—
who's dizzily spun and sung,
who's busily eaten rows of unhatched flies,
made footprints on the beach unmatched in size.

Soon the sun will rise on the horizon.

Eyes glitter in the woods and blink;
they're watching you, the groggy grizzly
who's snooped and snacked and had a drink.
And gotten soggy.
And now is pooped and ready to roam home.

You're a bear who rustles
deep in fallen leaves to rest
your muscles.
Lumber to your hidden lair to slumber.

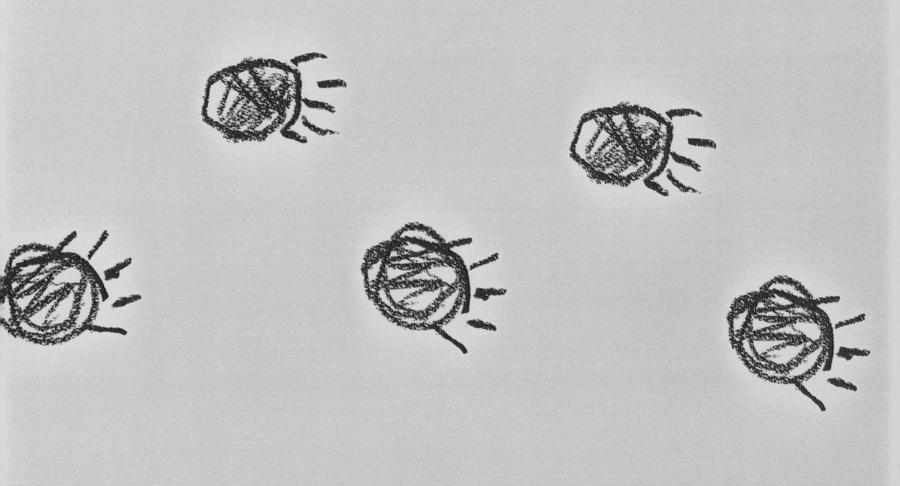